BUNS TRAVELS ACROSS AMERICA

Thanks to Gillian Meharg, Ann Marie, Dolores and Edward Love for helping immortalize my journey.

Cotton Tale Press

PO Box 470275

Fort Worth, Texas 76147

ISBN 1-881274-01-2

Sixteenth Printing

visit Buns' website:
www.bunsbunny.us

BUNS TRAVELS

ACROSS AMERICA

By Cottonpaw

Photography by David Love

COTTON TALE PRESS

Hi, I'm Cottonpaw. That's my name because my left front paw is as white as cotton, but everyone just calls me "Buns." I was born deep in the heart of Texas in a town called Waco. I was just like other rabbits until one day, I got a "hare" brained notion to go traveling. My adventures have taken me to many famous and wonderful places. I'll bet I'm the best traveled bunny in the whole U.S.A.! I wrote this story so boys and girls everywhere could learn, as I did, about America.

Statue of Liberty
New York City

I rode the ferry to Liberty Island to see a lady 300 feet tall. She was a gift to America from the people of France in 1886. The Statue of Liberty is the symbol of freedom around the world!

USS Constitution
Boston, Massachusetts

I peeked over an anchor and spied "Old Ironsides."
The ship got this nickname because cannonballs
bounced off her sides during the War of 1812.

Niagara Falls
U.S.A. and Canada

At Niagara Falls, the rainbow lasts the whole day long and stretches all the way from the United States to Canada!

White House
Washington, D.C.

This is where the President lives. The house was burned by British soldiers in 1812. It was painted white to hide the fire marks and has been called the White House ever since.

Lincoln Memorial
Washington, D.C.

President Abraham Lincoln worked throughout the Civil War to preserve the Union. His statue seemed so real that I cocked my ears to hear him speak.

Gulf Coast

I got my first taste of seafood at the beach on the Gulf of Mexico. It was DELICIOUS!

Bayou
Louisiana

You never know what you'll run into when you travel. Deep in a Louisiana bayou, I saw a scary looking ALLIGATOR! Do you see him? I'm lucky he didn't see me!

Mississippi River

I cruised up the Mississippi, from New Orleans to St. Louis, on a paddlewheel steamer. The captain told me the Mississippi is the longest river in North America.

Gateway Arch
St. Louis, Missouri

I lay on the grass and gazed at the Arch which soars 630 feet into the sky. All the carrots in creation couldn't keep me from hopping through this Gateway to the West!

I thought I saw a buffalo.

I DID! I DID!

On the grasslands of Oklahoma

Johnson Space Center
Houston, Texas

I spent a lazy afternoon at Mission Control and daydreamed of being the first rabbit in space.

The Alamo
San Antonio, Texas

Alamo means "cottonwood" in Spanish. It reminds me of my cottontail. The most famous battle for Texas independence from Mexico was fought here.

Pikes Peak
Colorado

The view from the top of this mighty mountain is all downhill. It was thrilling to know I was the highest rabbit in America!

The Grand Canyon
Arizona

If my ears were a little bit longer, I would fly the ten miles across to the other side. The Grand Canyon was carved by the Colorado River which flows a mile below my paws!

Saguaro National Monument
Arizona

Although I had never seen them before, I felt right at home among the saguaro cactus of southern Arizona.

Monument Valley

Monument Valley is on the border of Arizona and Utah. These buttes are named Left-Hand Mitten, Right-Hand Mitten and Merrick. Can you guess which is which?

Yosemite National Park
California

The spray from Yosemite Falls showered my dusty coat and washed my paw and tail as white as cotton! Can you find me?

Hollywood, California

I hopped down Hollywood Boulevard and discovered the star for my hero, Bugs Bunny. Do you think Buns will ever be as famous as Bugs?

Golden Gate Bridge
San Francisco, California

My journey had taken me from the Atlantic coast to the Pacific coast. As I looked back toward the east, I thought of all the wonderful places I had been in my travels across America.

I wonder where I will be tomorrow . . .